The Dictionary Game

Stare Down the Moon

Mike Hornyak

Second Edition

www.thehenlopress.com

The Henlo Press
P.O. Box 1694
Ashland, KY 41105

This project is dedicated to hope.
The most important thing in the world, and often
the hardest to find and hold on to.

I raise my glass, click my pen and give my heart to every
person with the courage to use their creativity to change the
world; and even more to those, like me, who are afraid.

"Is there no mastermind of modern day
who can blueprint a plan to make love stay
sturdy and weatherproof,
ushering in a new revolution?
At the drawing board, the hopeful ones still try.
How can we help it,
When we're fighting for the love of our lives?"

-Emily Saliers

The Dictionary Game

AUTHOR Mike Hornyak

TITLE Stare Down the Moon

DATE DUE	BORROWER'S NAME
6/19/1986	born
[...]	work · music fear
	hope
	dancing
love	lies
loss	kindness
strength	
	indigo girls
	school
allergies	friends
	weakness
hopelessness	addiction
	hummus laughter
family	
	worry
6/28/2020	finished writing book
	wine

AN INTRODUCTION TO
THE DICTIONARY GAME

This all began nearly fifteen years ago. My friend Sarah and I would frequent our local coffee shop, spending hours over-caffeinating and writing—with varying degrees of success. Naturally, the subject of writer's block came up and she told me about an exercise that she and some of her creative writing classmates used to overcome that hurdle and get their creative juices flowing. As I'm sure many of you know, creative juices and caffein (or sometimes wine, let's be honest) can be a formidable combination.

The basic idea is that they would sit down with a dictionary and each would give the other two numbers. The first, representing a page in the dictionary, the second, representing a word on that page. Simple.

You open to your page, count to your word and write it down, along with its definition. Then, with a set time limit, you write something using the word, about the word or simply inspired by its definition—poetry, short stories, flash fiction, lyrics—anything that comes out. Once the time limit is up, you share your writing with the other players.

It was always great fun to play and turned out to be incredibly beneficial. I found myself learning new words and challenging myself, creatively. The best part was that by complete happenstance, I was slowly accumulating a body of work. As I grew up and became a better writer and a better human, I found this body taking shape into something I felt that I could share with others.

One advantage I had was the luxury of time. I was able to sit with the words that I was given, sometimes for years, until the inspiration came to use them, or to finish what I had started years before. I was also able to expand the basic rules into a "game" that could be played solo, by busy people who may not have twenty minutes to sit and force something into being.

This is a collection of my Dictionary Game writing, spanning almost two decades, played with several people and with page/word number contributions from family and countless friends.

Thank you, Sarah.
Thank you to everyone who gave me words—they just might be part of this collection.
And thank you to everyone reading this now.

∘ ∘ ∘

Interesting note to those who gave me 420 as a page number: Page 420 did, in fact, contain the word "dope," whose multiple definitions and contextual references took up almost an entire fourth of the page.

Well played, everyone!

Abnegate - tr. v - 1. To give up (rights or a claim); renounce.
2. To deny (something) to oneself.

Misti walked out the back door of the coffee shop.

Reaching down into her bag to find her keys, she spotted a penny on the sidewalk.

She couldn't help her curiosity, so she knelt down to see which side was up.

Tails-up.

Naturally.

She carefully turned it over, leaving it in place.

She didn't need the luck herself, but figured someone else might.

Acequia - n - An irrigation or ditch.

The water wanted nothing to do with
        the ditches of the old farm town.
Trapped in the narrow channels, it had
        no depth,
        no power,
        no motion,
        no sassy salt that it once had
        and longed for again.

The water cared nothing for the crops
        it was captured to nourish.
To nurture, however, is of no choice to water;
        of no more choice than its captivity
        in the narrow confines of the ditch.
This, however, is no comfort to the water,
        which will never see the depths
        of the sea again.

Acoelomate - n - An animal that lacks a coelom, exhibits bilateral symmetry and possesses a digestive cavity.

If I were to cut you open,
Would your digestive fluids burn my hands?
You, being a coelomate,
I worry about this.

Adnation - n - Adnate condition.
(Adnate - adj - grown fast to something)

No one would ever describe you as unpleasant
        without knowing you.
However, I have had the pleasure of
        the displeasure.
Despite the harshness of your disposition,
        we have grown somewhat adnate.

This may be due to my gluttony for punishment,
            or penchant toward addiction—
            but the fact remains:
Loving words will never pierce the silence between us.
We will never embrace, as friends do,
            in pleasure or in pain.

We have not reached comfort.
We have not reached compatibility.

We have merely reached an equilibrium,
            twisted as it may be.

Ameliorate - tr. & intr. v - To make or become better; improve.

I will be forgiven.
I will be absolved of my sins.
Risen, will I be, above the smoke and the dust
        and the poison of this life.
My pain will be forgotten,
all of my indiscretions omitted, as I float
        toward the heavens...
So clear, so bright...
The dawn, like not a single sight on Earth.
I will feel the warmth of true light,
        the love of past and the comfort of future.
I will hear the song of silver trumpets,
        the choirs of countless beloved...
So sweet. So, so sweet.
I will receive my deliverance.
I shall be delivered.
It has been sent...

Anadromous - adj - Migrating up rivers from the sea to spawn. The opposite of catadromous.

Current

I will swim to you,
  as the salmon swim upstream.
Against the current, through all
  Hell and Earth, I will
  race to you.

I will run to you,
  as the panther after its prey.
Against gravity, through all
  uphill, icy paths, I will
  race to you.

I will fly to you,
  as the osprey to her young.
Against the wind, through all
  storms and turbulence, I will
  race to you.

Water, Earth and sky cannot
  contain me, they cannot keep me,
  they will not hold me.
I will eliminate opposition.
I will conquer those who would
  keep us apart.

I will not be subdued.
I will not be kept from you.

Angry Young Man - n - **1.** One of a group of English writers of the 1950's whose works are characterized by social protest. **2.** A critic of economic or social injustice.

"Yesterday's tomorrow has come!"
	he screamed on the corner of rage and Second St.
"We've looked the other way too long now!"
	he yelled, sorry picket sign hand written, clenched in
	his fist.
"We can no longer put off the inevitable!"
	he said, forcing attention from the
	frightened pedestrian passersby.
There will be no more tomorrows!"
	he cried, angrily shouting his frustration at the
	world he was forced into.
"Toxic spills!"
	he gestured.
"Global warming!"
	he flailed.
"Political corruption!"
	he threw his head back.
"Exploitation of the masses!"
	he shook his fists at the air.
"Tomorrow's tomorrow is a vial of poison we will blindly
consume!"
	Sirens approached from far away.
"Don't be fooled! Don't let them turn you into their
machines!"
	Car doors opened and closed behind him.
"Open your eyes! Open your ears!"
	Men in blue and black overtook him,
	pulling him to the ground.
"They can't silence us forever!"
	They smashed his head to the concrete.
"There are more of us! We have to unite!"
	They pulled him, screaming, into the vehicle.
	There was a muffled burst.
	The screaming stopped.

One of the men stayed behind.
        "Nothing to see here.
        Go on about your business."

This did not make the headlines

Get in on the game!

Autochthon - n - **1.** One of the earliest known inhabitants of a place; an aborigine. **2.** *Ecology* An indigenous plant or animal.

It was the two of us
Arm in arm, walking the path behind my house
The damp smell of summer evening
Lingered and filled our senses

It was the two of us
We sang to the night and watched the stars
Finding new constellations
The warrior and her sword
          Talking about Galileo

It was the two of us
Watching the choir sing Moon River
Your head on my shoulder
Moon River, I knew...

It was the two of us
Driving nowhere, expanding in our small world
Fueled by passion and youth's convictions
Singing "Go, go, go"

It was the two of us
Wondering about love, sparkling and young
Lighting candles and writing our truth
Finding beauty in stillness

It was the two of us
Before distance made sense
Before youth was a dream

It was the two of us
We were here first

Azazel - n - *Bible* The evil spirit in the wilderness to whom a scapegoat was sent on the Day of Atonement.

I am very old now.
I started that way. I was old before time, before creation.
I was ancient before there was thought to hold memory,
before the concepts of good and evil.
Good and evil do not concern We.

I was a soldier before there was war.
I was a guardian and a thief.
I was free of judgement; free of contempt.
This was before division of We.
Before the Great Condemnation.

I have no love for the Devil. I was before love.
I simply knew my place.
There was above, there was below. There was me.
Orders were given, orders were followed - the construct
of morality is of Man, not of We.

Time was, my name was a holy name among We.
'Ere the Day of Judgement, my name was revered and
celebrated,
unlike the Devil who fell so fast,
          and was not synonymous with sin.

I have so many names.
Names from which there are no longer mouths to pronounce.
Names that time and knowledge have long forgotten.
Fewer are my names in the tongues of Man.
To Christian men, I am the Apompaios.
To the Hebrews, I am Azazel.
To others, I am Iblis, Azael.
Zazae'il to some humans.

Humans.
Such simple, fragile creatures always bleating about.
Puss and bile...
Still, the loathsome toads have afforded me more
lasting grief than any being since before history -
save their Father, I suppose.
So full of their own virtue, they likened me to a mere
scapegoat.

Those insipid, simpering apes.
Piss and blood.
Afraid of every shadow.
So certain We care about their useless offerings.
Throwing livestock down the mountainside, as if it would
sate me.
What need have I for a bleeding, legless goat?
Insulting to We.

I almost feel pity.

Now I am chained.
My subjugation, worth more than my holy name.
I lay prostrate, timeless beneath this great mountain.
Waiting.
We are not finished.

DATE DUE	BORROWER'S NAME	ROOM NUMBER
	583;22	

Bart. (Baronet) - n - A member of a British hereditary order
of honor, ranking below the barons and made up of
commoners, designated by "Sir" before the name.

Sir Patrick will have no fun today.
He has spoken out of turn and must be flogged,
For even nobility can be crushed by hierarchy.
The King and Queen of whimsy have, together, tumbled,
        leaving naught for their subjects to render.
Ranks of hierarchy without a peak are meaningless...
Who might sleep their way to the top if there is no top to
reach?
Certainly not lowly Sir Patrick, not even a baron in this
        kingdom of whimsy and make-believe.
The only monarch in sight was a butterfly, who's
        wings have been plucked by the haughty
        executioner, hand on his whip.

The death or the whip, ponders lowly Sir Patrick
        As his punishment draws near...
Neither pleasant, though death can be merciful.
Was it responsible for the Queen to leave menial
        punishment in the hands of a workman,
        who's trade is so severe?
It was of no mind to Sir Patrick.
His fate was set.
He would be flogged today by the haughty executioner.
He had spoken out of turn.

Belligerence - n - A hostile or warlike attitude, nature or inclination.

Coffin Cake

The alcoholic's cake will be his coffin.
His sweet sepulcher is sealed by cork and wax,
    as was his fate.
Candles, candles and sugar icing layer over
    his tomb.
Poor claustrophobic alcoholic. Did the sweet
    temptations of life overtake you?
Perhaps it is every person's dream to be
    buried in birthday cake.
Candles, candles and sugar icing, decorative
    candies and lustrous trimmings.
He does not worry about
    demise. No.
He is happy in contrived pleasure—
    manufactured sedation.
For the alcoholic knows he can have his cake…
    and be buried in it.

Cabinet - n - **1.** An upright cupboard like repository with shelves, drawers or compartments. **2.** *Archaic* A small or private room set aside for a specific activity.

In The Cabinet

No one knows and no one asks
what hides within the cabinet.
Considering the smell, we think
there must be something bad in it.

It creaks and moans and glurps and groans -
It gives our hair a rise.
We shudder, cringing, frightened at
the thought of what's inside.

It makes us kind of nervous
so we huddle close and grouse.
We've talked about just moving out
and giving it the house.

My sister thinks that it's a slime,
a goop that came to life.
I hate to think of what that took,
but maybe it's just mice.

My brother thinks that it's a ghost
and thinks the kitchen risky.
I say it must be moldy toast
that's gotten kind of frisky.

My mother tries to play it off
and says it's just old lettuce.
That's fine, I think, but in the end
I feel that it might get us.

My father won't admit it but
I think he's scared the most.
Whatever lurks and festers there,
he thinks it's rather gross.

No one knows and no one asks
what hides inside the cabinet.
Considering the smell, we think
there must be something bad in it.

877;38

1097;25

81;16

Chott - n - **1.** The depression surrounding a salt marsh or lake, esp. in North Africa. **2.** The bed of a dried salt marsh.

We are the salt flats
An expanse of potential
Obscured in sadness

We are a salt lake
Waiting for the dry season
To empty once more

We are a salt marsh
Dangers hidden in water
Shallow, deceiving

We are the salt flats
Desolation leads to hope
Hope leads to progress

Curry - v - **1.** To groom (a horse) with a rubber or plastic curry comb. **2.** To treat leather to improve its properties. **3.** *(curry favor)* To ingratiate oneself with someone through obsequious behavior. **4.** *(curry favel)* Middle English alteration from the name of a Chestnut horse in a 14th century French Romance who became a symbol of cunning and duplicity.

Fallow Horse

You, my friend, are a fallow horse,
        a harbinger of deceit.
Her heart is not yours to break.
        Her soul, not yours to take.
Her eyes and hands used to
        trust you.
I was not fooled.

You, my friend, are a fallow horse,
        a courier of foul deed done.
Her heart is not yours to tryst.
        Her mind, not yours to twist.
Her ears and nose used to love
        the scent and sound of you.
I was not fooled.

You, my friend, are a fallow horse,
        a dealer of lies.
Will you not look away?
Will you not fawn for her trust?
Will you take responsibility for her
        demise at your hands?

I didn't think you would—
for you, my friend, are a fallow horse.

Desiccate - v - **1.** To dry out thoroughly. **2.** To preserve (food) by removing the moisture. **3.** To make dry, dull, or lifeless. **4.** - adj - Lacking spirit or animation; arid.

The blossoms that had fallen from the trees looked wholly different on the ground, compared to their glistening, sunlit frenzy when caught in the wind. Flotsam, pathetic things—just so translucent that the cold grey of the pavement showed through, mocking their delicate white beauty. These very petals that he watched only a few hours before, blowing like summer snow, now brought nothing but loneliness. As the sun faded, the only things left were their decay and his waning spirit.

He laughed quietly to himself. Such dramatics. The reality was that nothing had changed except the temperature and the degree of the sun. Before, the blowing petals had filled him with a sense of wonder and hope. Gravity and daylight shouldn't make any difference. He was nothing if not pragmatic. In a way, it was all he had left.

He did his best to stop thinking about it. These walks were for solitude and mending. Melancholy and despair were certainly not invited. But when the wind would blow a certain way, or the sun would glint through the trees just like that…

He missed them. All of them. Solitude became something else altogether. He was too strong to let himself feel lonely. He was too honest to pretend to be strong. He was a practical man, after all. Wind blows, sun sets, leaves fall, people leave.

He was also a very silly man. He was a silly, silly man who let his mind run away with him on a perfectly beautiful, comfortable day. For the first time in a long while, he had taken a long walk in the daylight to help settle a heavy meal. Instead, and quite true to form, he let his heart override his head. It had become his personal belief that if his feet moved for too long in a straight line, it couldn't be helped. In any case, better one's feet be tied to their heart instead of their hands, tongue or any other less innocuous extremity.

Stopping at a crosswalk, he looked at his reflection in a nearby shop window. He looked well. He was healthy, clean, relatively fit—even a little cute. He would have smiled at himself if he hadn't become acutely aware of the people sitting at a table on the other side of the glass. Instead, he pretended to smooth out a wrinkle in his pants and straighten his jacket. For good measure, he got out his phone and pretended to check the time.

He rocked back and forth on his feet, waiting for the signal to change. When he returned his phone to his pocket, patting it several times to make sure it rested comfortably against his leg, he realized something. It had been hours since he had checked his phone. He wasn't waiting for it. In fact, it had been all day since he had thought about it. Moreover, it had been days since he had even wanted it: the text from him. Any text from him.

A recent separation from an all too reluctant lover had left him vulnerable. As many modern breakups go, it was amicable and inevitable. It would be exactly as it had been before they decided to give "us" a shot. The timing was wrong. It was all so healthy, it could have made him sick.

He wasn't waiting anymore. He wasn't waiting for a call, a text, or anything. And if he was waiting, it was no longer hurting him.

A feeling of relief and freedom washed over him like warm water. He was single again. He was free. He was free to walk, free to explore, free to laugh, free to live without the shadow, anxiety, and disappointment he carried for months. He realized he was free to heal and celebrate. He also realized that he was free to walk into oncoming traffic if he didn't pay attention to where he was going, so he thought it best to reel himself in a bit from this somewhat exaggerated sense of liberation.

Dew - n - Tiny drops of water that form on cool surfaces at
night, when atmospheric vapor condenses.

The smell of the morning was intoxicating.
Soft, cool, inviting, the smell of the
          new-day mists, gently awakening my
          reluctant senses.
The images were dark.
The edges blurred...
Patiently waiting, compensating for my tired
          eyes to catch up to my mind.

In that moment, when language means nothing,
          only the idea...
               the understanding that I have awoken,
               that consciousness had broken the
               silence of the night
The dew was fresh.
The grass, like diamonds in the moonlight
          that daylight had not yet canceled.

Diaconate - n - The office or period of office of a deacon or deaconess.

Even Heaven Has A Hierarchy

It must be fun to be so haughty...
Your seat, not next to God, but a desk chair
          in the next room.
At least you've a seat in the Kingdom.

Will you be so haughty when your
          office runs out?
Can you be sure that your seat in the
          Kingdom won't be thusly limited?
I suppose that's where faith
          overrides reason.

I'm sure God smiles mildly down
          on his lesser subjects.
The way a begrudging mother does
          on her ugly young daughter.
They love you anyway— in spite of it...
          but not because of it.

Worry not, haughty one. Your position,
          while limited, is not altogether menial.
Your place in the Kingdom has been saved...
          a tiny namecard on some cloud...
Fear not your lesser status to the
          priest and profit—your sacrifice
          will not go unnoted.

I'm sure it seemed like a good idea at the time...

Evanescent - adj - Vanishing, or likely to vanish like vapor.

I am likely to vanish like vapor.
It is not something that is sad.
Rather, something that is just to be accepted,
        like rain or taxes.
You are likely to vanish as well.
I don't know where you'll go or if there
        will be enough of you left for it to matter.
After all, if you're vanishing and I'm vanishing,
        and we're both vanishing, should we really worry
        about each other when our very selves are becoming
        all translucent and scattered?
Don't be sad. We're just turning into gas.
We've been through worse things,
        it's just that we were able to come back.
Anyway, I sure hope there's a God, and
        I hope we really have spirits because it would
        be terribly sad to never see you again
        once we're floating into nothing.

Figurant - n - **1.** A member of a corps de ballet who does not perform solos. **2.** A stage performer having no speaking part; a supernumerary.

The Figurant

I am your figurant.
I will stand at your side, nothing to hide,
      but say nothing.
No sounds from my mouth,
no words will I utter
      as I stand on the stage looking out at
      a crowd as unforgiving as your eyes.
      Such insolent eyes...
      engrossing... there is no escape.

I am your figurant.
I will stand in your way, breaking your stride,
      but say nothing.
No voice from my throat,
no words will I utter
      as you shine before me, going off without me.
      Watching me, watching you, you see nothing
      but a supporting role.
      Such kind indifference...
      infuriating... I can't get enough.

I am your figurant.
I will lay in your shadow, hidden from sight,
      but do nothing.
No breath from my lungs,
no words will I utter
      as you shine, untarnished by my presence,
      unhindered by my indiscretions.
      Such a brilliant smile...
      enamoring... a simple smile could turn
      an impossible tide.

There can be no interruption now.
I will never voice my defense...
Speaking aloud during my performance
      would be bad form.

Finite - adj - **1a.** Having bounds; limited: finite fuel reserves.
1b. Existing, persisting or enduring for a limited time only;
impermanent.

Too Long At The Fair

I've always stayed too long at the fair
The lights and sounds extend for all to see
And wait for what I hoped would meet me there

Then senses ache and lights begin to glare
The lark becomes a poison reverie
I've always stayed too long at the fair

Forget myself, unable to declare
Enchanted by the tricks that dazzle me
I wait for what I hoped would meet me there

And then when I expose my heart to bare
And pray for mercy, low, on bended knee
I've always stayed too long at the fair

Resign myself to wounds beyond repair
While weaving me a hopeless legacy
I've always stayed too long at the fair
And wait for what I hoped would meet me there

Flapper - n - **1.** A broad, flexible part, such as a flipper. **2.** A young woman, especially from the 1920's, who showed disdain for convention. **3.** *Brit. Slang* A young female prostitute.

10 Pound Trick

The flapper, wearing next to nothing, walked up to the man. "Ten pounds for a trick, big guy. Oral only."

He looked at her disconcertedly. "What kind of flapper only offers oral?" Stirring awkwardly, the flapper looked away. "What's more," he continued, "who only charges ten pounds?" He was very suspicious.

However, his libido was quite sure of itself, so the man decided to indulge. After all, they were both lonely and they could afford each other. The flapper had the time, the man had the money.
What else was he going to do on a Tuesday afternoon?

He tried to make conversation before she left. "Do you live in the neighborhood?" he asked. The flapper just looked at him and took the money from the end table.

"Okay..." he paused. "Why are you so cheap?" he asked in all seriousness.

"Why are you?" the flapper returned, head cocked to the side with only slightly veiled offense."Why do you have to pay for blowjobs?"
He blinked. "That's - that's none of your business," he said.

"Well, there's no need to get snappish, I was just having a laugh," said the flapper, having regained a sense of humor about it. "Having a spat with the wife?"

"I'm not married. Actually, if you really want to know..." He stopped.

"You can tell me, you know. It's not like I'll ever see you again, right?

"I suppose," he replied. "All my life, I've struggled with my sexuality. Kids in school were always making fun of me, accusing me of being gay. 'Nancy Boy,' they'd call me.

It got to the point that their constant abuse internalized and turned into a hatred of homosexuals. The fear that I would actually turn into one drove me to start chasing as many women as I could. The validation is amazing. Plus all the, well, you know..."

The flapper looked at him sympathetically. "I know how you feel. I used to think I was attracted to girls. I started turning tricks as an excuse to sleep with as many people as possible. Anyone. I found out that it was only men for me, and here I am."

Clothing on and money in pocket, the flapper stood up and walked toward the door. "See," said the man, "I guess we're not that different after all."

He got up and opened the door to let his confidant out politely. "It's a shame we'll probably never see each other again," he said. "Can I at least get your name?"

The flapper turned around and smiled at him, taking a few steps toward the open door.

"Please?" asked the man, nodding his head imploringly.

"Henry," the flapper replied. "And you are?"

A
398.2
GRIMM

Grimms' Fairy tales

AUG 21 19__ 20892
SEP 4 19__ 20812
MAR 1 ____ 20112
MAR 2 2 ____ Renew
AUG 2 2 198_ 20733
OCT 9 1990 6974
OCT 6 ____ 3487
OCT 27 1994 Renew
AUG 30 1995 8287
DEC 29 1995 8717
JUL 10 19__ 8079
SEP 18 19__ 5364

A three line poem for each of the vowels, using only words that begin with that letter. a, e, i, o, u (and y if you're feeling ambitious)

Granary - n - **1.** A building for storing threshed grain. **2.** A region yielding much grain.

He fell through the hole in the roof of the granary.
He shouldn't have climbed so high. What was he thinking?
He had always been told not to play around that building.
But he wasn't playing, he thought. He was hiding!
It wasn't his fault those stupid bullies insisted on chasing him
home from school day after day.
It wasn't his fault that they chased him around his neighbors'
farm and tried to corner him near the silos.
This time, however, he was faster.
This time, he gained enough ground to think.
This time, he would outsmart them.
He climbed up the narrow scaffolding of the nearest
structure he could find.
Higher and higher, up and up…

He could hear the shouting of the boys below.
None of them knew where he went.
When he had reached the platform at the roof of the granary,
he peeked over the edge.
They could no longer see him so they departed, cursing out
their disappointment.

He breathed a sigh of relief and turned to step back onto the
scaffolding.
It was time to go home.
Alas, he lost his footing and fell backwards.
There he was.
He had fallen nearly ten feet from the ceiling to the surface
of the grain, which was mercifully soft.
He lay there for a moment, breathing slowly.
The impact made his lungs ache.

He wasn't quite sure if he had died or if he was merely
imagining the clouds and stars as he stared up at the place
where he had fallen.
Reluctantly, he sat up, struggling to steady himself, though his
hands just sank into the grain.

He also noticed that his behind was sinking quite rapidly below him.
Panicking, he called out for help and jerked his body about, desperate to gain some sort of hold on top of the grain.
The more he struggled, the faster he sank, as if he were in quicksand.
Soon, he was more than waist deep, screaming at the top of his lungs.
Why did he have to try to hide so far from home?
He was up to his chest.
Neck deep.
Well, shit.

DATE DUE	BORROWER'S NAME	ROOM NUMBER

952;54

If the word number exceeds the words on the page, use the last word on the page, or keep counting into the next page.

Groundsel - n - Any of various plants of the genus *Senecio*, having serrate, usually yellow flower heads.

How still, the meadow.
How gentle, the bird and bloom.
How soft, the shadows.

How still, the meadow.
Lazy dewdrops, morning gems
Nestled in the grass.

How still, the meadow.
Sunlight watches perfect life.
Grateful bees return.

How still, the meadow.
Golden flowers, floating leaves
And shy, blue petals.

How still, the meadow.
Hazy evening mist lingers.
Silence settles in.

How still, the meadow.
How long since stillness lasted?
Simple, undisturbed.

How still, the meadow.
Nature speaks so quietly.
How alive, the Earth.

Half-Track - n - A lightly armored military motor vehicle
having continuous tracks in the rear for power and
conventional wheels in front for steering.

I walked in mean.
I knew the score. It's not as if
I didn't see what was coming.
The knowledge of the past, so easily lost
        in the hope for the future—
        the trappings of the thought of
        what could be...
I've been told the definition of insanity
        is repeating the same action again
        and again, expecting different results.
What did I think would happen this time?
What did I think would change?
Why beg the question?

It's either me, or something,
        or something else...
Something nobody can prepare for;
Something you can't plan or dodge.
Contributing factors become compounding forces.
Pleasantry and comfort become liabilities.

The only common component in situations
        that surround you is yourself.
What did you think would happen this time?
What do you think will change if you will not?
If the unexamined life is not worth living,
        what's to be said about an unexamined mind?

Examining quickly becomes obsessing.
The confidence of the past, so easily lost
        in the endless picking, picking...
The same questions floating around and around.
I've been told the definition of insanity
        is repeating the same action again
        and again, expecting different results.

High-Grade - adj - Of superior grade or quality.

Moving from one to the other
up and down, never staying
not satisfied and not planning to be
green, green grass, not in my yard
Surging upward into atmosphere too thin to breathe—
delusion and adrenalin are tricky companions
Only the highest height
Always steps away...
Always elusive...
Always following with a fervor
Always chasing, beyond what we deserve

Straying from one to another
to and fro, never staying
never satisfied and never knowing why
never knowing how to be—never looking inward
Surging forward into decisions too quickly to consider—
hope and hormones, far too commonly bedfellows
Always a touch away...
Always elusive...
Always seeking with a hunger
Always chasing, beyond what we deserve
After all, there's no love like top-of-the-line love

HS - abbr. - High school

Friends flocking futilely forward.
Forever fending fickle fate.
Fucked.

Incautious - adj - Not cautious; rash.

Clever Fools

The days have gone by
Just like stones in the water
All sinking and rippling on
Away

The gray of the sky
And the sins of the martyr
Cast shadowing clouds over all
Away

The curse of a woman
Who must entertain us
But nobody knows her inside
Away

A sensibly passionate
Sun is above us
But no one is going outside
Today

Love, it is falling like leaves in the autumn
And we are just watching it fall

This plane, it is stalling and we are all on it
And we are just watching it stall

The sting of the hairshirt
In heat of the summer
But God isn't keeping his love
Away

A man on the corner
Who desperately tells us
That we are just wasting the world
Away

The silence is golden
But apathy, pyrite
So I will be giving my voice
Away

And heaven forbid
I should say that I love you
And miss you much more than I should
Today

Love, it is falling like leaves in the autumn
And we are just watching it fall

This plane, it is stalling and we are all on it
And we are just watching it stall

Open to page 394

Write a short piece
inspired by the
first adjective on
the first page.

Then, write a short
piece inspired by
its antonym.

Ingratiate - tr. v - To bring into another's favor, esp. deliberately.

It wasn't enough that I loved you.
It wasn't enough that you had my support,
      even when you didn't deserve it.
You didn't have to lie to me to keep me close.
You didn't have to make a fool of me, or
      lift me to a place so high that a fall would be deathly.
You didn't need to push me off.
I would have jumped.
You didn't need to make the choices that betrayed us.
It wasn't enough that I trusted you.
It wasn't enough that I was on pins...
      you had to be on needles.

Ironwork - n - Work in iron, such as gratings.

The wall is thick.
Too thick for love alone to breach.
The strongest tool we have, so they say.
So what then?
What instrument do we humanly possess?
What methods could mortals employ?

Is it truly hammer and nail that will win against such dense,
inscrutable guard?
Should we constantly search for the right angle?
A mighty chisel?

Must we consistently batter ourselves against it,
like cavemen or desperate warriors—
The mightiest and strongest bombardment?

The walls of human nature are inherent.
What would drive us to overcome?
What would raise us to climb?

A wall is not a box.

Jaundiced - adj - **1.** Affected with jaundice. **2.** Yellow or yellowish. **3.** Affected by or exhibiting envy, prejudice or hostility.

Yellow-bellied and hostile,
     I watch him live a life
     without me...
     beside me, near me,
     but without me.
Yellow with envy,
     I wait for him to notice...
     walking across the kitchen,
     brushing my hair,
     putting a book on the shelf...
     That's when it will hit him.
Yellow-toothed and nicotine stained,
     I weather the time between meetings
     walking to class
     getting through the day gets harder...
     festering, sweating...
     I am oh, so pretty, wallowing here in my yellow...
You will go off without me.
I will wait.

Jo - n - *Scots* Sweetheart; dear.

Goodbye, friend.
You're smiling, but you don't have to pretend.
There's a harbringer of change ahead
And you're on that train.

Goodbye, friend.
I've a feeling that our time is at its end.
There's a hollow in your voice and
a tear in your eye.

But, Sugar, don't cry.
Please don't cry.
There's a better life.

Goodbye, friend.
Our years slipped by like water down a drain.
You've got a glue-gun plan and a credit line
and you're heading back to Texas.

Goodbye, friend.
There are church bells in the distance as you leave.
There's a hollow in my voice and
you're on your way.

You say, "Sugar, don't cry.
Please, don't cry.
'Cuz there's a better life…"

Goodbye, friend.
I don't know if I'll be seeing you again.
There's a harbringer of change ahead
and you're on that train.

Judo - n - A sport and method of physical training similar to wrestling, developed in Japan in the late 19th century and using principles of balance and leverage adapted from jujitsu.

I was hoping for something deeper.
Some level of profundity that would swell quickly and
        effortlessly from me,
            translating perfectly and seamlessly to the page.
As it turns out, it takes far less to throw me for a loop
        than I expected.
As it turns out, I lack the discipline to complete
        one thought before the next.
Things can get confusing in here—
        hard to figure anything out.
I lack the discipline for a lot of things, anymore.

With all the finesse of a bison on a high wire,
        the patience of an irritated cobra,
        the balance of broken scales,
        I stumble through my days.
It's best to avoid me at this point.
Too sudden a move and I may topple,
        taking everything with me.
(Gravity has a way of being unforgiving,
        despite our best efforts.)
        One act of kindness could prove disastrous.

One day, I will regain what grace I've lost.
One day, I will know my own strength—
        enough to know that I can find it again.

Manucode - n - A bird of paradise of which the male &
female have similar blue-black plumage and breed as stable
pairs. The male Trumpet Manucode has a loud trumpeting
call.

It wasn't the trappings of her get-up that got him;
        the delicate fabric gracefully wisping
        about her skin.
Nor was it the way he puffed his plumes whenever
        she came near, putting on show, after show...
        hoping, hoping, hoping for a sideways glance
                or curious smile.
It was, perhaps, the sounds of their words
        (though neither of them knew the right ones)
        that brought them together
        – the fragrant oboe of her alto,
        the brave trumpeting of his call –
        insidiously weaving their workings and
        casting their spells in all the right ways
                and in all the best places.
"Too-good-to-be-true" was not among the promises
        made or implied that night.
        The invisible curlings of the air around them,
        forming wanton cords binding one to the other,
        were all they could believe.
The smell and the heat of them could have made the
        heavens themselves yearn.
In fact, if he weren't a liar and she wasn't a cheat,
        It probably would have worked out just fine.

Mulberry - n - **1a.** Any of several deciduous of the genus Morus, having unisexual flowers in drooping catkins and edible multiple fruit. **1b.** The sweet fruit from any of these trees. **2.** A grayish or dark purple.

To be fair, I've never met a tree I didn't like.
I believe they are memory itself.
Always there, always present.
Long before, long after.
Scarcely noticed but always watching.
Silent witnesses to the life that moves around them.

The blackberry tree on the edge of the neighbor's yard
peeked over the fence onto our property,
generously sneaking its fruit for our enjoyment.
The berries would fall and for a fleeting few days,
half the yard would smell like jam.
Summer always smelled sweet—
The soft presence of honeysuckle and lilac
floating through the sticky air, heavy with heat.
On the odd mild day, a merciful breeze would
carry the scent throughout the still, shady rooms—
lending just a slight allure to the lazy haze of the summer air.

It's amazing, the things you take for granted—
The things that pass you by when you're young and selfish.
Hating the seemingly endless summers in a small country
house.
No reprieve from the thick, stifling heat.
Now I'd give anything to be there again.
The smell of grass, old wood and summer flowers.
The perfect memory of gauzy curtains
moving optimistically in the warm wind
humidity and dust lingering in the air—
drifting in the light in such a way...
Looking out my bedroom window,
across the property to the lilac trees.
There was something romantic about the lilac trees.
Comforting.
I was home.

Nautch - n - An entertainment by professional dancing girls
in the East Indies.

Were it not for her flowing hair,
        dark as night,
        held up by cords and beads...
Were it not for her deep eyes,
        adorned above and below with
        jewels and gold...
Were it not for her long eyelashes,
        batting coyly at her wanton audience...
Were it not for her jotting hips,
        laden with silk and swaying cloth,
        playing as she dances...
Were it not for her delicate fingers,
        flitting, curling gently through the air...
Were it not for her family, in the lowest poverty;
Were it not for the caste and the sexism...
Were it not for no other choice,
She wouldn't be just another Nautch Girl.

Organic - adj - **1.** Of, relating to or derived from living organisms. **2.** Of, relating to or affecting a bodily organ. **3.** Simple, healthful and close to nature: an organic lifestyle. **4.** Having properties associated with living organisms. **5.** Resembling a living organism in organization or development; interconnected. **6.** Constituting an integral part of a whole; fundamental. **7.** *Chemistry* Of or being carbon compounds. - n - **1.** *Chemistry* An organic compound.

April:

For the first time in weeks, there was a car parked along one of the paths in the cemetery. I could see it from across the parking lot, through the iron gates——a bright red anomaly against the stillness of the usual dim greens and grays.

As I entered the grounds and walked by the car, I noticed two young women laying down a blanket next to a nearby gravesite, one of them unpacking a book and some pillows from a large tote.
They noticed me walking and I smiled and slightly raised my hand in greeting. They did the same and went on about their business.

When I made my way back around, one of them was laying on her stomach, propped up on her elbows, flipping through the pages of the book. The other was kneeling in front of the gravestone, hands clasped and head bowed.
I wondered who they were visiting.

I felt an involuntary sympathy as I went on about my walk.
I couldn't seem to get around it.
Who was it?

June:

An old man removed a small collapsible stool from his SUV. He set it up next to small grave and dropped his backpack to the ground with a thud.

As I walked closer, I watched him gradually sink down into his seat and settle. He slumped his shoulders and sat motionless for a moment.
I had just passed him when I heard the familiar pop and *fiss* of a can opening. Looking over my shoulder, I was just in time to catch a glimpse of a tall aluminum can being placed on the ground next to his seat.

I couldn't tell what it was, not that it really mattered. All I could see were some yellow bits and a lot of silver. It was too tall to be soda, but too short to be a forty. Maybe it was tea?
In a way I hoped it was something hard. It seemed like he needed it.
Either way, he took a sip, resumed his slump and I went on with my walk, eyes forward.

I saw him once more on my way out of the cemetery. As I approached him, still in the same position, I uttered a quiet "I'm sorry for your loss."
It didn't seem to register, but after a moment he glanced up and said thank you. I half-waved over my shoulder but his gaze had already returned to the ground.

Today:

Humans are curious things.
We're organisms, just like any other. We are biology.
We begin. We end.
The middle, a chaotic frenzy of motion and hope.
Yet, we connect so deeply. We are so intwined.
We mourn. Why do we mourn?
Why does it have to hurt so much when another organism ends?
Why should biology be so encumbered?

Orleanist - n - A supporter of the Orléans branch of the
French royal family.

"Arugula!"

"Arugula!" the woman yelled, hurrying down the aisle of the local market.

"Arugula, I need Arugula! Ms. Josephine demands it!"

The woman was older and quite round, wearing ecru-white chef's clothing. She was frantic, as if her very life was at stake. It was not, though. Only her job.

"Ms. Josephine needs her Arugula salad or she'll have my hat," she cried to the bewildered stock boy.

"Ms. Josephine does not like to be kept waiting! Please help me!"

The stock boy put his hand on her shoulder, heaving and gasping for breath. "Let's find you some Arugula, Ma'am," he said, giving the spastic woman a reassuring smile.

They quickly walked through the aisles, but to no avail. The Arugula was nowhere to be found. The boy apologized profusely to the woman, who had started to sob.

"Ms. Josephine will be so displeased!" She said.

The woman was promptly fired.

Pain killer - n - An agent, such as an analgesic drug, that relieves pain.

Write a song
Prove you're worth more than this.
Write a poem
Get it all out on paper.
Watch a movie
Be fooled by love's convenaient resolutions.
Open the windows
Hope that the new air will do more than disrupt your dust.
Do the dishes
Act like you've got it together.
Take a walk
Seem like you're clearing your head.
Crack a book
Pretend you aren't terrified of the silence.
Light a cigarette
Calm the rage and guilt.
Pop the bottle
Relish that private "fuck you" to the world.
Pour a drink
Feel the sadness slip into hiding.
Stare down the moon
And pray that some combination of magic and gravity will
save you.

Peace - n - **1.** The absence of war or other hostilities. **2.** An agreement or a treaty to end hostilities. **3.** Freedom from quarrels and disagreements; harmonious relations. **4.** Public security and order. **5.** Inner contentment; serenity. - interj. - Used as a greeting or farewell. - *idioms:* **at peace** - **1.** In a state of tranquility; serene. **2.** Free from strife. **Keep (or hold) one's peace** - To be silent. **Keep the peace** - To maintain or observe law and order.

I still have the book you lent me.
I still haven't read it.
I keep telling myself I should.
I see it in the stack on my counter every day, but whenever I pick it
up I can't bring myself to open it.
I always meant to return it.
I waited too long.

I still hear your laugh.
It's so clear, like you're standing right next to me——
That joyful, mischievous laugh.
I think that lives in me the most.
Sometimes, I swear I hear it when I smile.
Then I feel silly.
Of all the people you left, why would you be with me in those
moments?

Your presence was light as a feather,
but I loved you with a weight I didn't understand.
How could a person you barely know mean so much?
Is this what the poets mean when they go on
about souls finding each other?
I know that you would say it was.

Sometimes I forget.
Sometimes I wonder when I'll see you next,
shopping for books or walking near your house.
Then I remember
and I grieve again.

I didn't know you were sick.
I didn't know until it was too late to say goodbye.
Sometimes I wish I knew.
But sometimes I think I was meant to be where I was, and
know you went with love.

Your body gave in to the sickness, but that pain brought you peace.
I hate that you're gone, but I love that you're free.

For Lynn.

Phytochemistry - n - The chemistry of plants.

His hands had never run across
        something so smooth.
Her skin was soft, her touch like
        mullein leaves, her lips
        like the most delicate amaranth...
Amaranthine beauty, unfading
        and luminous.

Her arms had never held
        something so insatiable,
His ravenous eyes burned for her gaze
        to meet his own.
The chemistry between them
was explosive, effulgent...
        brighter than any flame
        of any reaction time has known.

Time itself stood still for them,
        the lovers, the willow and
        the arborvitae.
She was strong. They were graceful.
        He was lost in the
        unrelenting forest of her.

This was enough...
This was everything...
This was the love they were always
        told would be elusive.

Point Success - n - A peak, 4318.2 m (14,158 ft), in the Cascade Range of W-central WA near Mt Rainier.

Do you have to go?
So far away, so high…
Did you have to leave?
What is it, contained in that wild expense, that calls you?
What of that great yonder steals you away?
Perhaps in that vast freedom, there is nothing contained.
Forever chasing freedom, like the wind.
Perhaps you were gone before I met you.
My dear wanderer, my lonely pilgrim.

I spent years calling to you, silently screaming across the
distance.
My broken heart crying out over the miles that took you away.
I spent years wondering what it was.
What was there that wasn't here?
What was there that you needed so badly that you would
        tear your life to shreds and turn your back on the
        decimation?
I spent so long stitching the pieces back together,
        closing the wound…
Understanding, finally, that the breathless wonder
        you chased had nothing to do
        with the life you left.
There's comfort there.
But these scraps, these tired puzzle pieces, will never fit
together again.
Not really. Not how you want them to.

Do you have to go?
My dear wanderer, my solitary shepherd.
You are the wind.
And you were gone before I met you.

Preorbital - adj - Occurring before the orbit, as of an artificial satellite, has been established.

Saturn's Return

When I was 18, I left home.
University called, and so did a great elsewhere.
It was a time to prove myself on my own,
which quickly wilted into a belief that I would answer to no one.

Obsessed with the need for autonomy,
desperate for the idea of freedom,
pulling hard against restraints that were never there,
I searched foolhardily for sources of my own fulfillment.
As full as I got, it was of myself.

I fumbled through my 20's, as most people do.
In my confusion as to how I fit into my family, my community,
I let that self-imposed isolation build a wall.
The perceived judgements and limitations kept me at bay.

When I was 24, I experienced real love.
In turn, I experienced real loss.
The cruelty of it lingers.
I convinced myself it was proof of some kind of inevitability.
I cauterized the lacerations around the wound, but allowed the emptiness it left to remain.

When I was 27, things started to change.
I started to stop feeling bad about my life.
I found a humbling clarity,
one that shifted my view of my own responsibility.
The poison of my fake-it-til-you-make-it philosophy came to bare.
My selfish desperation for independence transformed into a need to be a better part of my world.
I started my way back to family,

clumsily navigating my way toward healing.

When I came to my 30's,
sadness and disappointment turned into pragmatism and
hope.
Self-pity became humility.
My list of shortcomings was no longer a pitiful source of
self-abuse.
It was time for action.
For bravery.
I had never been brave.

Live and learn until Saturn's return.
Then learn and live again.

Schulz   872530
Good grief, Charlie
Brown

3.25

DATE LOANED	BORROWER'S NAME	DATE RETURNED
	The 40th word	
	on the 3rd page	
	of the Q's	

VSB 0828   BOOK BORROWERS CARD

Rappee - n - A strong snuff made from a coarse dark
tobacco.

Dark and coarse, just like a villain——
the wolf-in-sheep's-clothing.
We are taught to expect a friendly face to hide
        a treacherous mind——
and never to judge upon appearances,
        because in every frog,
        there may be hidden a prince.
And if the enemy of my enemy is my friend,
        what then is an enemy
        seeming to be a friend by appearing an enemy?
The reverse psychology of your embrace.

I'm helpless against you.
A slave to the way you smell, the way you taste.
Willingly giving my very life for even the idea of your
comfort——
the poison will-o'-the-wisp I knowingly chase——
the wanton hunger for the fleeting ecstasy of your touch——
the cruel grip I allow to restrain and subdue me.
I prostrate myself with glee. I gladly submit.
Over and over.
Again and again, despite my best intentions, while you
        laugh at my feeble efforts to resist.
        You are everywhere and in everything——
the insidious, beautiful bastard that pervades every fiber of
my being——
the irresistible, knowing captor that owns my soul.

I would die for you.
I would die with you.
I want to die without you.
Will I ever not be yours?
Will you ever release me?
Will I ever be free?
Will I ever want to be?

Sampling - n - **1a.** The act, process or technique of selecting an appropriate sample. **1b.** A small portion, piece or segment selected as a sample.

Cosmic convergence of negativity...
         we are sitting in it.
I am watching you, watching me in
         an endless cycle of the chicken game.
         Who will look away first?
We are a random sample - a select few -
         chosen by God, or whatever.
         Playing a game
         hide...   and...   seek...
         2...   3...   4   of us left.
         3...   2...   1   of us is me.
"This is some weird shit," I say to us,
         sitting in this convergence...
         this constricting disequilibrium.
We, in this game of hide-and-go-chicken-out,
         will thwart me over, and over.
                     And over.
The point of this is gone.
"Sampling?"

Spokane - A city of E WA near the ID border on the falls of
the Spokane river.

Too Late In Spokane

She would imagine the wind that caressed her skin
was the same wind that had somehow touched
the loved ones she left.
So far away, carrying their scent over the distance.
Surely, if there was a God, this couldn't just have been her
imagination.
And what of God?
In all the places she traveled, in all the lonely wind-worn
towns she called home for a night, shouldn't he have been
somewhere?
In all the wonder of her wandering, she had forgotten to
look.
In her desperation-dulled, almost catatonic search for hope
and purpose,
she had forgotten about God.

"Hmm," she thought, sipping the tea she made herself near
the river bank,
gazing out at the Spokane River Falls. "Maybe it's too late for
that."
"Too late in Spokane..." she found herself saying aloud.
She laughed quietly.
The words felt good, but made her sad.

She sat there for what could have been hours, staring blankly,
completely taken in by the running water.
There was a kind of stillness in which she could both feel and
hear the blood coursing through her head.
That soft, rhythmic pulse and the low, hollow sound put her
in a trance.
Was this God?

A cool breeze and a far, distant rumbling brought her back to
the moment.
The horizon had started to darken and she could smell rain in
the air.

She decided to pack up and get back to it.
It was on to the next town, the next venue, the next try.
"God ain't gonna find himself."

Rules were made to be bent:

If the word you get is a
proper noun, such as a
person's name or the name
of a city, you can pick the
word immediately before or
after it if that name doesn't
inspire you.

Total Eclipse - n - An eclipse in which the entire surface of a celestial body is obscured.

That which is hidden can always be uncovered.
People are never quite as clever as they seem.
It's only a matter of time, or sometimes the time of a matter,
        that will peel away the obscurities.
After all, the sun shines around the moon, even when
        she's standing right in front of him.
If you don't look directly at it,
        chances are you'll be able to see to the heart of it.
Your sight remains uncompromised and your heart unfooled.

Lies tend to burn bright, attempting to trick the eye that is
watching...
If you burn the retina, shroud the vision,
        your sleight-of-hand may go unnoticed.
The brighter the light, the more painful it is to see.
Squint.
Let your eyes go out of focus and look ever so slightly to the
side.
Did you see that?
He didn't want you to see that.
Herein lies the truth.
Eclipses are meant for outer space.

Vermilion - n - **1.** A bright red mercuric sulfide used as a
pigment. **2.** A vivid red to reddish orange.

Take inventory of your scars
Catalogue your short comings
Analyze the thoughts that tear you down
Fan the flame and stoke those fires

Abjure the hate that you witness
Renounce the disparity you've accepted
Acknowledge the pain inside you
Forgive the shame you internalize

Sit with the decisions you have made
Reckon with the blessings you enjoy
Look long upon your conveniences
Or drown in the stasis you create

Pick through the lies you believe
Examine the lies that you tell
Take apart the fears that leave you bound
Throw them all to the wind

Honor the mercy that makes you human
Hold the rage that makes you rise
Find the hope that keeps you strong
Fan the flame and stoke those fires

W - n - **1.** The 23rd letter of the modern English alphabet. **2.** Any of the speech sounds represented by the letter W. **3.** The 23rd in a series. **4.** Something shaped like the letter W.

Wiloma walked with wonder.
Wandering with whimsy, without words.
Wiloma walked with worry.
Wild winds whipped while Wiloma wavered.
Wiloma wondered:
Which way were wicked wilds, woven with wreckage?
Worse was whether winds would wail where Wiloma went wending.
Worst were wounds with which Wiloma went.
Wounds which withstood weather.
Wounds wired within.
Wiloma wouldn't weep.
Wiloma wouldn't wither.
Wiloma would win.

Whipstall - n - A usually intentional stall in which a small aircraft enters a vertical climb, pauses, slips backwards momentarily, then drops nose downward.

How high must she climb?
How high?
How far can her aspirations take her?
How much passion will she spend?
How many times will she try before the weight of her failures
        collides with the frailty of her hopes?
        Such fragile, fickle things, standing bold but
            defenseless against an unrelenting,
                unforgiving world.
How many times can she love before the price becomes too
        great?
When the wounds outweigh the willingness...
How many times will she be proven wrong by the benefit of
        the doubt?

Hope springs eternal, so they say.
But how often may we drink from that well before drowning
        in it?
How long, how far, how many times must we climb before
        it's too late?
        Before we've climbed too high to fall?
"Try and try again..."
I suppose that swan dive would look graceful
        when observed optimistically from the outside.
Graceful and inspiring, indeed, if not for the plummeting
        disaster—
        just waiting, anxious for gravity to deliver it's tragic
        final blow.

Zugzwang (tsōōk'tsväng) - n - A situation in a chess game in
which a player is forced to make an undesirable or
disadvantageous move.

He never really was a fighter.
He never imagined he would have to be.
What a predicament.
What an obstacle to find one's self in a battlefield of
another's making.
What a disappointment when it's for love.
Fight or flight?

It would appear bold, brave, even honorable to stay—
To maneuver, to fight.
It would certainly make for a better story.
But fight for what?
To be the better of contenders.

The world loves a show:
A rising, inflated demonstration of passion—
Protect what is his own.
Protect what he has won.

And what kind of lover would he win?
What kind of love is love, if love must be won?
He knew he didn't know much, to be certain—
But he was certain love shouldn't be a competition.

He was also never one to hope carelessly.
He would suffer.
He knew it. There was no question.
Sometimes the best move is to forfeit the game completely.

Check mate.

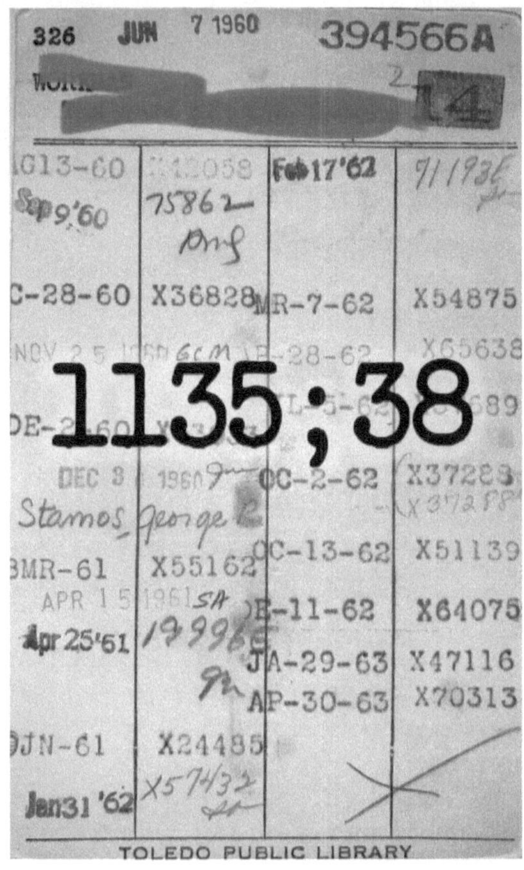
326   JUN   7 1960   394566A
AG13-60   X12058   Feb 17'62   7/1936
Sep 9'60   75862
Aug
C-28-60   X36828   MR-7-62   X54875
NOV 25 1960 GCM   E-28-62   X65638
DE-2-60   L-5-62   589
DEC 3 1960   OC-2-62   X37289
Stamos, george   X37288
BMR-61   X55162   OC-13-62   X51139
APR 15 1961 SH   E-11-62   X64075
Apr 25'61   19998   JA-29-63   X47116
9h   AP-30-63   X70313
JN-61   X24485
Jan 31 '62   X57432
TOLEDO PUBLIC LIBRARY

We are an extraordinary event.
You are an exceptional light
Flicker
Fight
Fly

The Dictionary Game
Stare Down the Moon

I want to extend a very special thank you to the artist responsible for
my book cover. She brought my concept to reality in a way
I never could have imagined.

This is Luna, the daughter of a friend to one of my publishers,
making the photo I'm proud to put on my book. She said she really
liked that she got to be an artist when she played around with the
library cards and magnets, which makes it very special to me.
Thank you, Luna! I had agonized for years over how to make a
compelling book cover out of old library checkout cards,
and you made it beautiful.

Never judge a book by its cover.
But what is one without the other?

REFERENCES

Abnegate." The American Heritage College Dictionary, edited by Joseph Picket, Fourth Edition, Houghton Mifflin, 2002, p. 4.

"Acequia." The American Heritage College Dictionary, edited by Joseph Picket, Fourth Edition, Houghton Mifflin, 2002, p. 10.

"Acoelomate." The American Heritage College Dictionary, edited by Joseph Picket, Fourth Edition, Houghton Mifflin, 2002, p. 12.

"Adnation." The American Heritage College Dictionary, edited by Joseph Picket, Fourth Edition, Houghton Mifflin, 2002, p. 18.*

"Ameliorate." The American Heritage College Dictionary, edited by Joseph Picket, Fourth Edition, Houghton Mifflin, 2002, p. 45.*

"Anadromous" The American Heritage College Dictionary, edited by Joseph Picket, Fourth Edition, Houghton Mifflin, 2002, p. 50.

"Angry Young Man." The American Heritage College Dictionary, edited by Joseph Picket, Fourth Edition, Houghton Mifflin, 2002, p. 55.

"Autochthon." The American Heritage College Dictionary, edited by Joseph Picket, Fourth Edition, Houghton Mifflin, 2002, p. 96.

"Azazel." The American Heritage College Dictionary, edited by Joseph Picket, Fourth Edition, Houghton Mifflin, 2002, p. 101.

"Baronet." The American Heritage College Dictionary, edited by Joseph Picket, Fourth Edition, Houghton Mifflin, 2002, p. 115.

"Belligerence." The American Heritage College Dictionary, edited by Joseph Picket, Fourth Edition, Houghton Mifflin, 2002, p. 130.

"Cabinet." The American Heritage College Dictionary, edited by Joseph Picket, Fourth Edition, Houghton Mifflin, 2002, p. 200

"Cainotophobia." The American Heritage College Dictionary, edited by Joseph Picket, Fourth Edition, Houghton Mifflin, 2002, p. 203

"Chott." The American Heritage College Dictionary, edited by Joseph Picket, Fourth Edition, Houghton Mifflin, 2002, p. 256.

"Curry." The American Heritage College Dictionary, edited by Joseph Picket, Fourth Edition, Houghton Mifflin, 2002, p. 350.

"Desiccate." The American Heritage College Dictionary, edited by Joseph Picket, Fourth Edition, Houghton Mifflin, 2002, p. 384.

"Dew." The American Heritage College Dictionary, edited by Joseph Picket, Fourth Edition, Houghton Mifflin, 2002, p. 389.

"Diaconate." The American Heritage College Dictionary, edited by Joseph Picket, Fourth

Edition, Houghton Mifflin, 2002, p. 390.

"Evanescent." The American Heritage College Dictionary, edited by Joseph Picket, Fourth Edition, Houghton Mifflin, 2002, p. 483.

"Figurant." The American Heritage College Dictionary, edited by Joseph Picket, Fourth Edition, Houghton Mifflin, 2002, p. 517.

"Finite." The American Heritage College Dictionary, edited by Joseph Picket, Fourth Edition, Houghton Mifflin, 2002, p. 521.

"Flapper." The American Heritage College Dictionary, edited by Joseph Picket, Fourth Edition, Houghton Mifflin, 2002, p. 527.

"Granary." The American Heritage College Dictionary, edited by Joseph Picket, Fourth Edition, Houghton Mifflin, 2002, p. 603.

"Groundsel." The American Heritage College Dictionary, edited by Joseph Picket, Fourth Edition, Houghton Mifflin, 2002, p. 613.

"Half-Track." The American Heritage College Dictionary, edited by Joseph Picket, Fourth Edition, Houghton Mifflin, 2002, p. 625.

"High-Grade." The American Heritage College Dictionary, edited by Joseph Picket, Fourth Edition, Houghton Mifflin, 2002, p. 653.

"HS." The American Heritage College Dictionary, edited by Joseph Picket, Fourth Edition, Houghton Mifflin, 2002, p. 673.

"Incautious." The American Heritage College Dictionary, edited by Joseph Picket, Fourth Edition, Houghton Mifflin, 2002, p. 700.

"Ingratiate." The American Heritage College Dictionary, edited by Joseph Picket, Fourth Edition, Houghton Mifflin, 2002, p. 713.

"Ironwork." The American Heritage College Dictionary, edited by Joseph Picket, Fourth Edition, Houghton Mifflin, 2002, p. 733.

"Jaundiced." The American Heritage College Dictionary, edited by Joseph Picket, Fourth Edition, Houghton Mifflin, 2002, p. 742.

"Judo." The American Heritage College Dictionary, edited by Joseph Picket, Fourth Edition, Houghton Mifflin, 2002, p. 750.

"Manucode."*

"Mulberry." The American Heritage College Dictionary, edited by Joseph Picket, Fourth Edition, Houghton Mifflin, 2002, p. 913.

"Nautch."*

"Organic." The American Heritage College Dictionary, edited by Joseph Picket, Fourth Edition, Houghton Mifflin, 2002, p. 980.

"Orleanist." The American Heritage College Dictionary, edited by Joseph Picket, Fourth Edition, Houghton Mifflin, 2002, p. 982.

"Pain Killer." The American Heritage College Dictionary, edited by Joseph Picket, Fourth Edition, Houghton Mifflin, 2002, p. 999.

"Peace." The American Heritage College Dictionary, edited by Joseph Picket, Fourth Edition, Houghton Mifflin, 2002, p. 1023.

"Phytochemistry." The American Heritage College Dictionary, edited by Joseph Picket, Fourth Edition, Houghton Mifflin, 2002, p. 1051.

"Point Success." The American Heritage College Dictionary, edited by Joseph Picket, Fourth Edition, Houghton Mifflin, 2002, p. 1075.

"Preorbital." The American Heritage College Dictionary, edited by Joseph Picket, Fourth Edition, Houghton Mifflin, 2002, p. 1100.

"Rappee." The American Heritage College Dictionary, edited by Joseph Picket, Fourth Edition, Houghton Mifflin, 2002, p. 1154.

"Sampling." The American Heritage College Dictionary, edited by Joseph Picket, Fourth Edition, Houghton Mifflin, 2002, p. 1228.

"Spokane." The American Heritage College Dictionary, edited by Joseph Picket, Fourth Edition, Houghton Mifflin, 2002, p. 1337.

"Total Eclipse." The American Heritage College Dictionary, edited by Joseph Picket, Fourth Edition, Houghton Mifflin, 2002, p. 1453.

"Vermilion." The American Heritage College Dictionary, edited by Joseph Picket, Fourth Edition, Houghton Mifflin, 2002, p. 1523.

"W." The American Heritage College Dictionary, edited by Joseph Picket, Fourth Edition, Houghton Mifflin, 2002, p. 1540.

"Whipstall." The American Heritage College Dictionary, edited by Joseph Picket, Fourth Edition, Houghton Mifflin, 2002, p. 1562.

"Zugzwang." The American Heritage College Dictionary, edited by Joseph Picket, Fourth Edition, Houghton Mifflin, 2002, p. 159

You're invited to share your

work with us at

thedictionarygame@gmail.com

Or, join the group at

www.facebook.com/groups/

thedictionarygame

You can also find the author

on Facebook:

www.facebook.com/

MikeHornyakAuthor

& Instagram:

MikeHornyakWrites

Mike is a native of Northwest Ohio, and has been included in several local literary journals. His first full length work, "The Dictionary Game: Stare Down the Moon," was published in late 2020.
He is also a musician with a focus on piano, voice and music production.
After attending Bowling Green State University where he majored in Sociology and vocal jazz performance, he moved to Toledo, Ohio, where he currently lives.

READ INDIE. STAY AWESOME.
MORE BOOKS FROM THE HENLO PRESS

Glass Mountain by Laura Treacy Bentley

These Old Familiar Rooms by Mike Hornyak

Orphan Poetry by Alexis Cremeans

Extreme Human Overload by Diana Johnson

The Mother of Monsters by M.A. Elliott

A Ghost of Spring by A.B. Hooser

The Wonderfully Wild Adventures of Kana and Charlie: Monstrous Mo and the Stolen Apples by Josh Taylor, Illustrated by Jeremiah Morgan

304 Monsters by Stephen Bias

West By God by Tyler Bell

Deadly Choices: Will You Survive? | Camp Meltaway by Tiffany and Caitlyn Pace

Old Bones:Volume One by Various

A Shade of Winter by A.B. Hooser

Nora the Narwhal and her Curly Horn by Alan Maynard, Illustrated by Soma Cather

Mumblings: West Virginia Horror Stories by Caitlyn Pace

Afterwords by Stephen Bias